4/13

D1367687

THE MYSTERY

AT

Fort
Sumter

Managing Editor: Sherry Moss
Cover Design: Vicki DeJoy
Picture Credits: Paige Muh
Content Design: Randolyn Friedlander

Gallopade International is introducing SAT words that kids need to know in
each new book that we publish. The SAT words are bold in the story. Look
for this special logo beside each word in the glossary. Happy Learning!

Gallopade is proud to be a member and supporter of these educational organizations
and associations:

American Booksellers Association
American Library Association
International Reading Association
National Association for Gifted Children
The National School Supply and Equipment Association
The National Council for the Social Studies
Museum Store Association
Association of Partners for Public Lands
Association of Booksellers for Children
Association for the Study of African American Life and History
National Alliance of Black School Educators

**America's National Mystery Book Series™
for Young Readers!
Where the Adventure is Real...and
So are the Characters!**

For more than 30 years, Carole Marsh has been creating
REAL KIDS REAL PLACES mystery books set in major
American locations and using real kids as characters in the
books. Readers of this popular national series can go
online to track the books they have read on a map! They
can also find a Scavenger Hunt, Pop Quiz, and other fun
activities to "Continue the Adventure!" Teachers can
download a REAL KIDS REAL PLACES Teacher's Guide,
an Author's Bio, Book Club Questions and Activities,
and more!

And just in case you want to know:
- YES! Mimi (Carole Marsh) and Papa (the cowboy pilot)
  are real!
- Christina and Grant are their real grandchildren! (So are
  Avery, Ella and Evan!)
- There is a *Mystery Girl*
  airplane...and a *Mystery
  Girl* boat (named *Mimi!*)
- And yes, kids can go
  online and apply to be a
  character in a future
  REAL KIDS REAL PLACES mystery and join the
  Fan Club!

Start your adventure TODAY at
www.carolemarshmysteries.com!

ABOUT THE CHARACTERS

Christina
Yother,
13, plays
Christina

Grant
Yother,
11, plays
Grant

Anna
Muh,
9, plays
Ashley

Rebecca
Muh,
7, plays
Cooper

Avery
Longmeyer,
6, plays
Avery

Ella
Longmeyer,
4, plays
Ella

Evan
Longmeyer,
1, plays
Evan

CHRISTINA yawned. It seemed so very strange. She and her brother Grant usually traveled with their grandparents to Charleston in the spring or summer. Yet here they were, creeping along at impossibly slow speeds down a dark, wet highway in the dead of winter.

They had left Mimi and Papa's Gullah blue-doored home in Savannah's historic district just awhile ago. Papa's big gray SUV had crossed the Talmadge Bridge and passed the South Carolina state line without incident. There was no one on the dark and mysterious road. The frozen trees hung low over the highway. It looked like they were driving through a dark, lacy tunnel. The full moon only now and then peeked down through the leaves like a big white eyeball spying on them.

Papa drove carefully, ever vigilant of icy spots that could send them careening off the highway. The thought made Christina shiver. She snuggled further down into the Clemson afghan Papa had tossed back to her when she complained she was freezing, despite the heat that was pouring from the vents. Across the seat, Grant hunkered over his video game, the greenish light from the monitor creating a skeletal glow in the car. Mimi was asleep.

They stopped at Green Pond to go to the bathroom. In the old store, Christina marveled at the array of enormous cooking pots and ladles. She wondered what kind of creatures you could catch in these low-country waters that would require such tools. Again, she shivered.

As they sped on toward Charleston, Christina read the curious sign names by moonlight: Ashepoo...Combahee...Edisto... Pon Pon Plantation.... Gray beards of Spanish moss swung from trees and even street signs. Ghostly shadows flickered on the road. It reminded Christina that Charleston was known as the Most Haunted City in America.

Usually that would be good news. Usually, they would be headed to Charleston in spring during the garden season when the

Spoleto arts festival was going on, or in summer to visit the beaches at Folly or Wild Dunes. Mimi would be working on a new kids' mystery book, and she and Grant would be helping her. But this night they were not headed for sun and fun—they were headed to a funeral. Mimi's Aunt Lulu had died.

To make matters worse, it was the Christmas holidays. They'd been visiting with their grandparents when the call came, which is why they happened to be cooped up in this cold car all glum and sad. So what kind of fun could this be? What kind of mystery adventure? What kind of Christmas?

Christina didn't even want to think about it. Of course, there was no way she could possibly know that it would turn out to be what she would later describe as "the worst one of all"...what Grant later called "the best one of all!"

Papa made an easy right turn and they faced a city glittering in the foggy cold. "Charleston," he announced.

Christina glanced at the car's digital clock: MIDNIGHT.

"Of course it is," she groaned, and hid beneath the afghan as the car bumped down an ancient cobblestone street into town.

1
"WHAT FORT IS THIS?"

GRANT yawned. When the car stopped, he looked up to see that they were parked in front of what looked like a grand fortress.

"Are we going to sleep at Fort Sumter?" he asked, yawning again. He turned off his video player, thrusting the car from green gloom to just plain old black gloom.

"This is not Fort Sumter," said Papa, stretching, his cowboy hat scraping the roof. "This is a hotel. It's the old Citadel building, and yes, the young men who once stayed here would say it is indeed a fortress." Papa laughed.

From the back seat, Christina and Grant stared at the edifice shrouded in fogged light, then stared at each other. They shrugged their shoulders.

"Looks like a fort to me," Christina whispered to her brother.

"Towers...turrets...gun ports..." said Grant. "Yep, looks like a fort to me."

A GIANT yawn escaped from the front seat. "Are we sleeping at Fort Sumter?!" cried Mimi.

She stretched and sat straight up, her short blond hair a spiky mess.

"Oh, for gosh sakes!" moaned Papa. "It's a hotel! Or, we can sleep in the car."

"Uh, no thanks!" said Christina, shoving the Clemson afghan aside. She gathered her things. "There is no bathroom in the car."

"Or television," reminded Grant, eagerly grabbing his backpack.

Papa opened the car door as a sleepy bellman in a uniform approached. "No TV. It's late. It's bedtime. Let's go, pard'ners—NOW!"

The kids, and even Mimi, "hopped to."

"Wow," Christina whispered to her brother. "Papa sounds like a drill sergeant or something."

"He's just tired," said Mimi. "That drive on slick streets is nerve-wracking."

"Mimi!" said Grant. "You were asleep...how do you know?"

Mimi turned around. Her eyes were still red from weeping over poor Aunt Lulu. "Now, Grant, you know how I have eyes in the back of my head?"

"Yes, ma'am," Grant said.

"Well, guess what?" said Mimi. "I can also 'backseat drive' your Papa from the front seat—even with my eyes closed."

Papa, who was holding her door open and offering her his hand, shook his head. "It's true, Grant, and don't forget it. You can't get anything past Mimi." He gave Mimi a weary wink.

Mimi smiled and perked up. She took his hand and hopped out of the car, following the bellman and their luggage cart inside.

"Well, do we even get dinner?" Grant asked forlornly. He rubbed his tummy and tried to look like a starving waif. He and his sister waited eagerly for the answer.

Mimi and Papa barely turned their heads around, but together they said, "NO!"

As Christina entered the spooky, fortlike hotel, she noted the time on the lobby clock.

"Forgetaboutit, Grant," she said sadly, putting her arm around her brother's shoulders. "It's closer to breakfast than dinnertime. I have some M&Ms in my backpack. We'll make do."

"Great!" grumbled Grant. "Next, I guess we'll find out we're staying in the dungeon?"

Papa hovered over the check-in desk. A skeletal-looking desk clerk handed him their room keys. "The room you requested, sir," they overheard him say. "The Dungeon Suite."

Christina and Grant exchanged shocked glances, and nervously followed their grandparents into the gloom of the darkened lobby.

2
TO THE DUNGEON

As they made their way through the spooky lobby and onto an elevator, Christina spied strange shadows dancing on the walls...or was that just from the candlelight? Tinkling water made her think of a drippy, old dungeon, but when the elevator doors opened, they found themselves in a regular hotel corridor. The bellman shoved the cart ahead of them and stopped at a door at the end of the hall.

"Room 13," muttered Grant. "Naturally."

Inside, the kids were happy to see that it was a two-room suite, so they had a sofa bed to pull out and their own television, and the fridge and microwave were in their room. Soon, and in silence, they had all gotten into their pajamas. Papa mumbled something that sounded like "Gunnite" and headed to bed. Mimi helped the kids manage the sofa bed, then curled up with them against a bank of pillows.

"So what happens next, Mimi?" Christina asked her grandmother, who still looked very sad.

"Not sure," said Mimi. "I haven't heard from Aunt Lulu in years. I only got one quick phone call about her death, from a stranger, so I don't really even know where to find her!"

Grant's eyes opened very, very wide. "So you mean we're going to have to search Charleston for a dead body?!" He scrunched down into the blankets.

"Grant!" squealed his sister.

"It's ok," Mimi assured him. "I am sad, but Lulu was very old. All her family died long ago, so that's one reason she was always so hard to stay in touch with. She really isn't even my aunt. I, uh, I think she's the aunt of my mother's third cousin once removed."

Christina and Grant stared at one another, then burst into laughter.

Now Mimi was offended. "And just what's so funny?"

"Sorrrry," sputtered Christina, and she and Grant burst into laughter yet again.
Mimi frowned, then laughed herself. "I know, I know," she said. "It sounds strange. But really, I had to come."

"For the funeral?" Christina offered somberly. She punched her brother to stop his uncontrollable giggling, especially since he was slobbering on her side of the covers.

"No," said Mimi, matter-of-factly. "There is no funeral. Lulu was cremated."

"Then...?" Christina prodded.

Mimi sighed. "I had to come for the reading of the will. It seems that my name is mentioned."

"JACKPOT!" cried Grant, giving a high-five sign to his sister.

"Knock-it-off, Grant!" said Christina, slapping a pillow at her brother's head and missing.

"Don't get your hopes up, Grant," Mimi warned. "I'm under the impression that Lulu lived a very modest life. She has probably left me something sentimental, like a vase or something. I only knew her when I was a very young girl."

"That's sad," said Christina.

"It was," Mimi agreed. "But Lulu was always the life of the party!"

Christina and her brother stared at one another, astounded. Very strange, indeed!

Suddenly, Mimi sat up. "Ok, now, it's very late. Get to sleep. We can only hope that we can pay our respects quickly, dispense with the will business and head for Savannah and then Peachtree City. Christmas is coming in a few days, you know, and we need to get home—I promised your parents and Uncle Michael and Aunt Cassidy, and Avery, Ella, and Evan are expecting you on Christmas Eve."

"So we don't even get to look around Charleston?" asked Christina. She was disappointed. She wanted to get home for the holidays, too. She was missing her friend's Christmas party, as it was. But she loved the old, amazing, historic town of Charleston and knew that it must be decorated big time for the holidays.

"Yeah," said Grant. "Papa promised he'd take me to Fort Sumter. We're studying the Civil War in school, you know."

Mimi did not say anything. She had snuggled back on a pillow and was sound asleep.

"Can we move her to her bed?" Grant asked.

Christina shook her head. "I think we had better let her sleep."

"It's just like one-hundred-and-one Dalmatians," Grant grumbled. "Too crowded in this sofa bed with girls and women."

"Then I have a very good idea," said Christina with a grin.

"I know, I know! You don't have to tell me!" Grant groaned, then grabbed a corner of the blanket and rolled up into it like a sausage and off onto the floor into an instant "sleeping bag."

They all dozed off so quickly that they did not hear someone enter a card key into their door. The door handle rattled and rattled, but the door would not open.

A light snow fell all night in Charleston.

3
FROZEN FORTRESS

The next morning, sun belted its way through the bars of the blind slats in the window of their room. "Ouch!" screeched Grant when he opened his eyes.

"Hey, what's this?" grumbled Christina, rolling over. Mimi was gone. Through the doorway, she could see her grandmother snuggled up to Papa. She had stolen all his covers. "We have a chance to sleep late and look at all this sunlight."

"I want to get up early," said Grant, popping up. "I'm starving! We didn't eat dinner last night, remember?"

Christina rubbed her stomach and hopped up too. "Oh, I remember, all right. We had a chorus of rumbling tummies in the night." She staggered over and opened the blinds. "Wow! Look at that!"

Charleston—specifically, Marion Square, a ten-acre park famous for festivals and concerts in downtown Charleston—was coated in a thin layer of ice. Everything glistened like a showroom of crystal. "Pretty!" said Christina.

"Slippery!" said Mimi, now awake and peering over her grandkids' heads.

"TREACHEROUS!" thundered Papa, rubbing his eyes, and startling them all.

A block of ice from a large tree limb crashed to the ground.

"Well," said Grant, "at least it's beginning to look like Christmas...instead of like a funeral."

In no time at all, they had dressed and headed up to the inn's indoor courtyard.

"How pretty!" squealed Christina, as she got off the elevator. She gallivanted around the indoor courtyard with its splashing fountain, Christmas trees, and old-fashioned gaslights, bedecked with holly and red ribbon.

In the meantime, Grant explored the curious corner staircases which spiraled up into turrets as tall as the building. "What is this place?" he asked Papa.

Papa stood tall. He had been in the U.S. Army and always liked to share military history with his grandkids. "This place has quite the military history that dates back to Revolutionary War times. It once housed tobacco, if you can believe that. Then it was used as an arsenal, a fort, and most recently as a military college. In 1911, it was named The Citadel, The Military College of South Carolina. Cadets proudly marched within these walls!"

Grant could tell from the look in his grandfather's eyes that he was envisioning the past right before his eyes. "That's cool," he said. "But can we eat breakfast now?"

Papa groaned. "Grant, one day you're going to appreciate history."

"I do, I do!" promised Grant. "Right before each social studies test I have to study for!"

Papa scrubbed Grant's head with his knuckles. "Grant, you are incorrigible!"

"No," argued Grant, pulling away, "I'm in...misery! Starving!" He grabbed his middle and staggered toward the buffet like a wounded soldier.

Mimi and Christina joined them. They went through the elegant buffet line and helped themselves to Charleston stone-ground cheese grits, mini-ham biscuits, scrambled eggs, bacon, fruit, muffins, and much more. Soon they were all settled in comfortable chairs beneath palmetto trees decorated with tiny lights.

"Well," said Mimi, solemnly, as they ate, "I guess we'd better get our chore over with first."

"Our chore?" asked Grant, puzzled. "We have to clean our own rooms?"

In spite of herself, Mimi giggled. Grant could always make her smile. "No, Grant," she said, "Housekeeping will do that. We have to find Aunt Lulu. You know, to pay our last respects."

"And then we might do some tourist stuff?" asked Christina hopefully. "Or even Christmas shop?" She knew King Street would be a fairyland of holiday lights and Christmas gifts.

"Probably," said Mimi, tugging her cell phone from her purse.

"And we men can go see Fort Sumter, right, Papa?" Grant asked in a deep voice.

"Uh, sure," said Papa. "We men can do anything."

Mimi and Christina rolled their eyes. "Then can YOU MEN go and fetch the sleigh and reindeer?" Mimi said sweetly with a smile. Christina giggled.

"We have a sleigh and reindeer?!" said Grant enthusiastically.

"I think Mimi means the SUV with the four-wheel drive," Christina said with another giggle.

Papa stood up. "I think what Mimi means is NOW?"

Mimi nodded as she punched in a phone number on her cell, and the men, with

Christina tagging along, headed through the lobby to get the car. They never knew how long Mimi would be on the phone once she made a call. But as soon as they pulled up in the SUV, Mimi was standing in the hotel doorway. She held her purse tightly and looked very troubled. Christina had a funny feeling that their plans for the day had just gone awry.

"What's wrong?" asked Papa, opening the door for Mimi. He already had her heated car seat nice and warm.

Mimi got in, settled back, and frowned. "Aunt Lulu," she said in a quiet voice, "is missing."

4
CALLING AUNT LULU

Just for a minute, Christina (who was always very observant, her grandmother said) noticed that the bellman seemed to be especially nosy about their business. He held Mimi's door open while he seemed to eavesdrop on this curious conversation.

"What do you mean?" asked Papa. "She's dead."

Mimi frowned. "I mean the funeral home says they've never received the body. So no one seems to know where she is. She's missing."

"Missing in action," muttered Grant from the backseat.

"Well, not exactly in action," corrected Christina.

"It's not funny!" said Mimi. "They should not have lost Aunt Lulu."

"Whoever 'they' is," said Papa.

"Well, they told me that they would contact me as soon as they located her," said Mimi.

"Well, they better, or else!" said Papa, as he started the car. With a strange look on his face, the bellman **reluctantly** shut the door and moved away just in time to avoid being pulled along with the car as Papa screeched out of the driveway.

Christina and Grant cringed. They knew when Papa said something like this he really meant it. "So what should we do in the meantime?" he asked gently.

Mimi sighed. "They have my cell phone number. So let's go see Fort Sumter before Grant croaks."

"Thanks, Mimi, but we don't have to," Grant said unconvincingly. Christina could see her brother had his fingers crossed hopefully behind his back.

"It's ok," said Mimi. "We might as well do something to take our mind off this mystery."

Papa frowned. "Please don't say the M-word, ok?"

"What M-word?" asked Mimi, innocently, though Christina and Grant knew Mimi knew exactly what Papa meant.

"The MYSTERY word," Grant volunteered.

"But we love a good mystery," Christina reminded them all.

"But maybe not this time," said Papa. "It's almost Christmas and we don't need any dead body mysteries. Actually, maybe for a change we don't need any mysteries at all." He glanced at Mimi hopefully. But since he had to watch the traffic and the slick streets, Papa never saw the tiny smiles that Mimi, Christina, and Grant each wore.

Slowly, Papa drove down King Street through the center of Charleston. The pretty street was lined with shops old and new decorated for the holidays in typical

Charleston style. Magnolia leaf wreaths encircled gaslight lampposts. Bright red velvet bows held up swags of Spanish moss entwined with twinkling white lights. Storefronts were filled with sparkly holiday party clothes, beribboned gifts, toys, stuffed animals, glittering antiques, chocolate-covered Yule log cakes, and ever so much more.

"Oh, Mimi," begged Christina, "can we please shop before we leave town?"

Mimi said, "I hope so, Christina. We'll see."

Christina did not like the "We'll see" term. She knew that's what adults usually said when they actually meant, "Don't get your hopes up."

Papa turned left onto The Battery and they drove along the waterfront. On the right was the cold, gray Ashley River, and on the left was a row of gorgeous antebellum Charleston homes, all decorated for the holidays like something out of a fancy Victorian-era magazine.

They wound over a cobblestone street, passed a park of white except for the black cannon and stacks of cannonballs. Papa turned their attention to the **bleak** island that held the famous Fort Sumter—the historic site of the firing of the first shot in America's Civil War (or War Between the States, as many Southerners called it).

"You can barely make out the island from here. It's about 4 miles out. We can get there by ferryboat, if you're up for it. Little chilly, though, if you ask me."

"It's perfect," argued Mimi. "It will take our minds off our myst...uh, I mean our problem, and besides, Grant and Christina can learn more about the Civil War. It says here to take Concord Street up to near the South Carolina Aquarium to what's called Liberty Square. There's a visitor center there. We can catch the ferry from there."

Grant grinned; Christina frowned.

Papa parked and they clambered out of the SUV and scampered toward the entrance to the fort's museum and the ferry dock. A frigid ride aboard the white-capped river took them to Fort Sumter. The fort looked bleak and sad this cold winter's day. Very few visitors mulled about.

"This is a national monument," marveled Christina. "Doesn't that usually mean it's a very important historic site in American history?"

"Oh, the Civil War was a very important period of American history. It was a brutal war, with brother fighting against brother. You'll learn more when we get inside." Christina noted that her grandmother looked very sad, and not her usual bright and sunny self.

"Yeah!" said Grant, as Papa motioned for them to follow him. "Did you know they didn't have any anesthesia back then? They just lopped off arms and legs left and right with no painkillers or antibiotics. I once saw a picture of a big haystack of **amputated** limbs in a Civil War book. How cool is that?!"

"GRANT!" Mimi squealed.

"How gross!" said Christina.

"There was nothing cool about the Civil War," Mimi reminded her grandson gently. "Even if some young, eager, idealistic soldiers thought so, they soon learned otherwise."

Grant was confused. Papa had been a soldier (not in the Civil War, of course) and Grant thought that was cool. Why was everyone fussing at him and contradicting him? What kind of Christmas holiday vacation was this, anyway? Missing dead aunt? Grouchy grandparents? Nasty, wet, cold, icy weather? And a really bad feeling that things were only going to get worse.

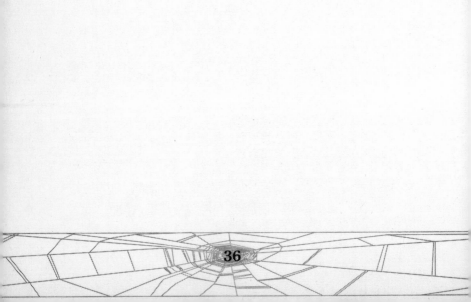

5
CIVIL WAR MAN

A man dressed in an NPS Ranger uniform greeted them. "Well, not too many folks about today!" he said merrily. "I guess I get to give ya'll the dee-luxe tour! Have a seat."

They followed his order and listened carefully as he gave a brief background at what had happened in Charleston Harbor a mere 150 years ago. His deep voice was mesmerizing and soon they were all riveted to his tale of war and woe:

"Just imagine it! Our nation was not even 100 years old yet, and it was about to go to war—with itself! A lot of people think the war was only about slavery, but it was also about states' rights. In November 1860, Abraham Lincoln was elected president.

"On December 20, when it was clear that Lincoln would assume his duties as president in March of the following year, South Carolina became the first state to secede from the Union! Who could even imagine the United States now breaking up into two separate groups? It was unthinkable, but it happened!

"After more Southern states left the Union, they formed a new government—the Confederate States of America—with Jefferson Davis as their temporary president. America was now two separate nations. What would happen?

"In spite of being in South Carolina, Fort Sumter was a federal, or U.S., fort. Confederate leaders demanded that the fort surrender!

"From April 12 to 13, 1861, Confederate troops bombarded Fort Sumter with cannon fire! The people of Charleston climbed onto the roofs of their houses to watch what looked like an explosion of fireworks. The 34 hours of fighting started the Civil War. Fort Sumter surrendered. Amazingly, no one was killed. But this was not the end—but the beginning—of a four-year war that killed more than half a million soldiers!

"Many of those killed were mere boys. Many times, brothers faced each other on the battlefields, and killed each other. It was the Confederates against the Union forces. One day, all had been fellow Americans. The next, bitter hatred divided them. It would be a long time before America was one country again. Questions?"

Mimi, Papa, Christina, and Grant sat speechless. Grant, especially, looked like he could cry. He hadn't really realized how horrible the Civil War had been. He tried to imagine his Uncle Michael shooting at his dad—how could something like that happen?

From behind them, a young girl raised her hand. "Tell them about the missing cannon balls!"

Her sister yanked the hand down. "Shush!" she said. "We're not supposed to talk about it, remember?"

Christina and Grant spun around to see what the two girls were talking about. Both were pretty, blond, pink-cheeked, and shy. The little sister was the one who had spoken and now she looked like she might be in trouble. They could see that the older sister was staring intently at the ranger. They spun around to look at him, and Christina could easily see that some secret communication had transpired, without either the man or the girls speaking a word. It was very suspicious!

The ranger sighed. "Well, it's no secret, not really," he muttered sadly. Then he explained, "For some strange reason, someone has been stealing cannonballs from the fort. And not just from Fort Sumter, but from other historic sites around Charleston that have cannonballs on display." He looked very aggravated.

The older girl spoke up. "Those cannonballs are priceless historic artifacts, you know!"

"It's a federal crime to steal that kind of thing!" added the younger girl eagerly.

"And who might you girls be?" asked Papa kindly. He was always the gentleman and never met strangers, only new friends, whether they were young or old.

Once more, Christina and Grant noticed the strange, secret, silent communication pass between the ranger and the girls. He had a stern look on his face like he was reminding them to behave, or hold their tongues, or something.

Finally, the older girl stuck out her pink-gloved hand. "Hi, I'm, uh, I'm Ashley!"

Grant nudged his sister in her side and gave her a look that silently asked, "What's up with that? Doesn't this girl know her name?" Christina just shrugged.

"And I'm Cooper!" added the younger girl, sticking out her pink-gloved hand. Christina noticed that the ranger gave them a "good job" nod.

"Hi!" boomed Papa in his deep voice. "I'm Papa, the cowboy pilot of the *Mystery Girl* airplane, and this is my family: Mimi, who writes kids' mystery books, Christina, our

granddaughter, and Grant, our grandson. Are you girls from Charleston?"

"Yes!" said Ashley at the very same time that Cooper said, "No!"

Now Mimi and Papa looked confused and the ranger groaned. Then he quickly changed the subject when a woman entered the room and called for the girls to follow her. "That's our mom," said Ashley, getting up.

"Are you sure?" Grant said, and now it was his sister's turn to punch him in his side. "Hello!" said the attractive woman, cheerfully, although it sounded a little fake. She seemed nervous. "Come along, now, girls, and let the tourists enjoy their tour. I, I mean, we have work to do."

Christina and Grant noticed that the woman wore a nice navy pantsuit that looked sort of military, not from Civil War days, but maybe like a Secret Service agent might wear. She also wore a small National Park pin on her lapel.

"So you work for the Park Service, too?" Mimi inquired pleasantly. Christina and Grant did not have to look at their grandmother to know that she had her "something's certainly curious here" antenna up. But the woman just huffed, "Not really," and turned on her heels, tugging the girls behind her. Mimi frowned.

Christina giggled. "No mystery, hey?" she whispered to Grant.

"Something's sure up," said Grant.

"I'm UP!" boomed Papa. "Let's get out and get some fresh air." He and Mimi headed off to look at historic displays.

Christina and Grant knew that their grandparents could stand there for hours and read every word on every sign, so they headed outdoors and never noticed the ranger give them a very "Evil Eye" look as they left the building!

6
WATCH YOUR SIX!

Fresh air is exactly what they got when they went outside. The wind had picked up and the air was icy. Since the fort was situated on an island, it seemed twice as cold as it had in downtown Charleston. Christina and Grant tugged their jackets closer around them.

Immediately, they spotted Ashley and Cooper over by a large, uncharacteristically giant-looking cannon on the far wall of the fort. Their mom seemed to be making some serious notes in a notebook and she took snapshots all around the cannon. The girls looked like they were just trying to stay warm. On the other side of the fort, Grant noticed a familiar figure. "Hey, isn't that the bellman from the hotel?"

"I doubt that seriously," said Christina, but she looked anyway, her eyes tearing from the cold air. "He doesn't have his uniform on."

"You mean he's naked!" squealed Grant, doing a double-take.

"No, silly!" said Christina, "I mean he might be our bellman, but he's wearing jeans and a jacket, not his bellman's uniform. Besides, it couldn't be just a coincidence that the bellman is visiting Fort Sumter on the very same day as we are, right?"

Grant sighed. "I have the same question myself. Hey, look at this!" he added, pointing to a row of cannon that had cardboard signs marked with numbers stuck down with duct tape beside them.

They both ran forward and looked closer.

"It looks like these numbered spots are where the missing stacks of cannonballs sat," said Christina. She pointed to the broken brick where it appeared something had been ripped up.

"So why is Ashley and Cooper's mother examining those spots so hard and taking pictures, too?" Grant asked.

"And why is the bellman, if that's who he is, following us around the perimeter of the fort wall?" Christina asked nervously. She looked back, but Mimi and Papa were nowhere to be seen. "Come on!" she told her brother. "Follow me!"

Slowly and stealthily, they made their way around the fort, pretending to read historic information, while really they were just trying to keep an eye on the mom and Ashley and Cooper ahead of them, as well as on the bellman following them. It was a slow, blustery dance, as they rocked first on their toes, then heels, trying to keep their balance in the whisking wind.

"What are Ashley and Cooper doing?" Grant asked.

He and Christina could see them hunkered down over something they seemed to be trying to hide. Their mother motioned for the girls to follow her, and with a quick glance back at Christina and Grant, they stuck their heads into the wind and trudged off toward the ferry landing.

"Wonder what that was all about?" Christina said, but her words were lost in the wind so her brother did not answer.

"Watch your six!" Grant shouted back to her.

Christina knew that this was Papa's military term for "watch your back." She spun around to spy the bellman—if indeed he was—gaining on her. He seemed to be moving faster, as if to catch up. Mimi and Papa were still nowhere to be seen. Christina guessed they were staying out of the wind. So she just tried to move faster and catch up with her brother.

When she caught up with him, near the fort's flagpole, she found him tugging at something stuck to the pole.

"What is that?" asked Christina. Surely her silly brother wasn't yanking on someone's old chewing gum?

"Come on!" urged Grant. "Follow me!" He moved quickly and Christina had to hurry to keep up.

He had tucked the object into his fist and glanced back nervously at the bellman, who gave the kids a dirty look.

7

THE CANNONBALL CAPER

"There you are!" shouted Mimi into the wind. "It's getting really cold!" "Let's get out of here, please."

Papa put his jacket around Mimi's shoulders and led her toward the ferry landing to the ferry. Christina and Grant tugged their jackets up around their necks and followed.

Christina and Grant purposefully dawdled behind their grandparents.

"Show me!" Christina insisted in a whisper.

Carefully, so that it would not blow away, Grant unfurled a piece of paper with a scrawl on it.

"It's parchment—with calligraphy writing!" marveled Christina.

"It's a clue!" Grant promised.

Christina shook her head adamantly. "No it isn't. You just wish it was. What does it say?"

Grant held tight to the paper as he read aloud, "Ask not who the bell tolls for...it tolls for you!"

"Bell?" said Christina. "Do you think that bellman left us this dumb clue just to scare us?"

"Ha, ha!" said Grant, grinning. "So you agree—it is a clue?"

Christina frowned. "I don't know what it is. I don't even know if it's for us. And I sure don't know what it means."

Grant spun around, his arms wide. "Not for us? Do you see anyone else here, sister?"

Christina glanced around. She had to admit that Fort Sumter suddenly seemed very lonely. In fact, it had a very haunted feel to her. She felt a sudden urgency to leave the island.

Just then, Papa motioned for them to come closer. They looked out at the whitecaps, then at the docked ferry. The waves were tossing the boat port and starboard in a topsy-turvy movement.

"Mimi won't like this ride," Christina remarked.

"Well, I will," said Grant, racing to join Papa.

"Why?" Christina called after him, feeling a little queasy just watching the angry sea.

"To get away from him!" Grant called back to his sister. He pointed and Christina turned to see the so-called bellman quickly gaining on her, a scowl plastered on his face. Just then, he slipped, but quickly regained his footing and hurried past her, face red with embarrassment. Christina exhaled with relief and caught up to the others, but not before glancing back in awe at a bit of American history and wondering where Ashley, Cooper, and their mom had gotten off to.

Papa herded them all aboard and quickly inside the ferryboat's glass-enclosed area. With the windows so steamy from the cold outside air meeting the warm inside air, they could not see if anyone else boarded, but if they had, they must be hanging around outside in the cold so as not to be seen.

"Grant!" hissed Christina. "Where's the cl..., I mean the note?"

Grant looked all around, dug in his pockets, and shook his head. "I don't know. I guess it blew overboard."

"It's ok," Christina assured her brother. "We know what it said."

"Yeah," said Grant, plopping down on a bench. "But not what it means."

Suddenly, Papa appeared with two paper cups of steaming hot chocolate. He handed each of them one and warned, "Watch your tongues, it's hot."

"Thanks, Papa," said Christina. A cup of hot chocolate was better than a pair of gloves or mittens any day, she thought. Papa nodded and headed back to where Mimi stared at a nautical chart of the river.

"Look!" said Grant, staring out the porthole window. A streak of whipped cream moustache curled over his upper lip. He rubbed the window clear with his napkin.

Christina peered outside. It was snowing!

"Imagine that!" she said. "I don't think snow is very common here, not even at Christmastime."

"About as common as clues stuck to a flagpole," muttered Grant. "And missing cannonballs from a national historic site. Not to mention a missing dead aunt."

What the two children did not see as they slipped outside into the light snow was the bellman hunkered down against the wind behind a pile of ship's mooring line...or Ashley, Cooper, and their mother chatting with the pilot in the pilot house.

Christina glanced back at Fort Sumter receding into the distance. "It must have been scary to man that fort and be bombarded by constant cannon fire," she pondered aloud.

"Yeah," said Grant, equally thoughtful. "I think I know how they felt. Under sea! Grant moved closer to the door, eager to get back inside.

Christina looked puzzled. "You mean under siege, don't you?"

Grant did not like to be corrected. "Under sea, under siege, under the weather, underwear—something like that."

"Don't worry," Christina said with a giggle. She slung her arm around his shoulders. "I know exactly what you mean, and how you feel."

"Misery loves company," Grant said.

Suddenly, Christina and Grant were startled by a giant BOOOOOOOOM!

Instinctively, both kids fell to the deck and wrapped their arms around their heads. The gigantic BOOM sounded exactly like cannon fire, only there were no cannon to be seen. And, no cannonballs to be fired.

Papa and Mimi appeared from inside to see what was going on. The bellman was now nowhere to be seen.

"What was that?!" Grant asked Papa as he and Christina regained their composure and stood up.

Is that cannon fire?!

58

Papa looked across the river and laughed. "It's a big freighter unloading its cargo," he said. "Look at that!"

The kids turned toward Charleston's aquarium on the nearby shore, and saw that just past it a row of humongous freighters from ports around the world were lined up at the dock. A skyscraper-tall crane snagged the big boxcar containers and stacked them on the dock like giant building blocks.

"Wow, that's cool." Grant tried to sound more enthusiastic than he really felt. Despite the relief he obviously felt about not being the subject of a cannonball attack, Grant still felt uneasy and stayed desperately close to their grandparents as they exited the ferry onto "dry" land.

8
RAINBOW ROW

Soon, they were tucked back into the SUV. Papa had the four-wheel drive on since snow was swirling all around them and the roads were slick. They headed back downtown to go see Aunt Lulu's lawyer.

Papa always chose to drive by The Battery, or Batt'ry as the locals called it, so they could see the water, and in the summer, the sailboats. Today, though, in the near-blizzard, they could barely see the water at all. Still, several older couples bravely hunkered into the wind for their late afternoon walk, and last-minute Christmas shoppers shielded their precious cargo from the snow.

"Aren't the Christmas lights pretty in the snow?" said Christina, scrubbing a clear circle in the frosted window with her finger. "Especially the gaslights."

No one answered, each seeming to be in their own private thoughts: Papa about the weather...Mimi about poor Aunt Lulu...Grant about the mystery that was a'foot. Even Christina found herself hypnotized by the falling snow. She couldn't help but wonder if they would get home in time to spend Christmas with the rest of her family. If not, it would be a first. Just the thought made her tearful, in spite of Charleston's magical beauty.

They passed the U.S. Custom House and the Old Exchange and Provost Dungeon. Soon, the SUV rumbled down a short, bumpy street of large cobblestones, once ballast in the holds of ships. Papa parked in front of a brick rowhouse where the owner lived upstairs and had his office downstairs. The shingle over the door read: John Thomas Tradd, Esquire, Attorney at Law.

Papa got out and went around to open Mimi's door. "Stay here a minute kids, and let's see if this lulu of a lawyer is home."

The interior of the car chilled the moment the motor was turned off. The kids waited impatiently—not that they were eager to visit a lawyer's office. It sounded like a place where you got bored, adults talked a lot, and your stomach rumbled loudly because you were starving, but no one seemed to care.

In a moment, Papa cracked the door to the office and motioned for them to come inside.

Grant and Christina groaned, but obeyed their grandfather and hopped out of the car. Inside it was warm—way too warm, like maybe a hundred degrees, Christina thought. John Thomas Tradd appeared to be about a hundred, himself. He and Mimi were talking softly, but Christina could see that the old man was shaking his head no. Papa motioned for them to sit down. Their grandfather kept standing, and it was his stomach that growled loudly.

The kids sat on a hard sofa that stuck their bottoms with itchy things, as if it were stuffed with horsehair. They hoped this would not take too long. It was sweltering in the small office.

Suddenly, Grant punched his sister in the side. When she turned to complain, he put his finger to his lips in a "Shush!" sign and motioned into the darkened inner office. The door was barely cracked, but they could both easily see the corner of what looked like a pine box.

"Is that a coffin?" whispered Grant.

"Surely not!" Christina whispered back.

Papa gave them a "Shush!" look, then turned back to Mimi and the lawyer.

On a nearby table, Grant found a piece of yellow legal paper and a pencil. He wrote: What if Aunt Lulu is in there? Should we say something?

Christina wrote back: No! It will upset Mimi. I see a business card on the table. We will call as soon as we leave and ask.

Grant beat her to the punch and reached in a silver seashell bowl to pluck out a card, only what ended up in his hand was another piece of parchment paper! As he reached to shake his sister's shoulder so she would look, Papa turned around, and instead, Grant began to fan himself like a little old lady at a funeral.

That got Christina's attention and she took the note from him. It read: Meet us at the Sword Gate House as soon as possible!

Christina and her brother stared at one another in amazement. Who had written this note? Why had they been to Lawyer Tradd's office? It was all very suspicious. And, they had no idea how they would get away from Mimi and Papa and go to that house—wherever it was. Another clue, but they felt so helpless.

Finally, Mimi stood up. "Well, thank you," she said. "This has been most helpful."

Even her grandkids could tell from her voice that what she really meant was, "This has been most un-helpful."

Papa took Mimi by the arm of her red suit and her blond curls shook as she sort of stomped out the door. The kids quickly followed.

It was silent in the car as Papa drove just a few blocks away to the busy part of Meeting Street. In spite of the snow, the restaurants and shops were aflutter with tourists and locals.

They parked and Papa led them to something wonderful—a warm, steamy restaurant smelling of hot hush puppies, oyster stew, steamed shrimp, and key lime pie! Soon they were seated behind the fogged windows and served big mugs of iced tea with lemon and mint leaves. Papa ordered for all of them since he knew their seafood favorites.

"What did the lawyer say, Mimi?" Christina asked, while they waited on their food.

"He was not helpful," her grandmother admitted. "He swore he had checked all the funeral homes and Aunt Lulu is nowhere to be found. He thinks it's just a mix-up, not any foul play, and he's called the police to help hunt for her."

No one knew what to say.

Finally, Grant blurted, "Maybe she's already been buried?"

Instead of being upset, Mimi snapped her fingers. "You know, Grant, you could be right! Maybe she was accidentally buried in error, which of course, just means some other poor person..." She did not finish her sentence, and fortunately, their food arrived.

As they ate, Mimi and Papa talked rapidly about what to do next regarding Aunt Lulu.

Now it was Christina's turn to punch her brother. "Look!" she whispered to him and pointed to a table across the room.

"Hey, it's Ashley, Cooper, and their mom!" Grant whispered back. "What are they doing here?"

Christina cackled. "Eating lunch, just like us, silly!"

But Grant still looked troubled. "Can I be excused?" he asked Papa, pointing toward the restrooms.

"Sure," said Papa, hardly turning around.

Before Christina could stop her brother, he hopped up and headed toward the other table. As he passed by, she saw Ashley drop a paper napkin on the floor. Deftly, Grant bent over and swooped it up. He headed on toward the restrooms, but just turned at the door and made a beeline back to their table.

As he sat down, Grant slipped the napkin to his sister. In a kidlike scrawl, it read: Meet us at the bookstore next door!

Christina and Grant stared at one another. The clues were piling up as fast as snow and they were trapped and could not get away. Just then Grant pointed out the now cleared window. A bicycle bell had caught his attention. When they looked, they both saw the bellman passing by on a bike, clearly watching them!

"What do you think?" Christina asked her brother.

"I think he really is a 'bell' man!" Grant giggled. "Get it, Christina, BELL man!"

Christina sighed. Bad things were going on and their mystery-loving and mystery-solving grandmother was going to be of no help at this time. How could her brother be so useless? How could things be so hopeless? And then to make things worse, Ashley, Cooper, and their mom got up to leave; the bellman passed back by, ringing his tinny bell again as some kind of warning; and Lawyer Tradd appeared in the doorway and asked for a table.

These girls are not clueless!

9
ASSIGNATION IN THE BOOKSTORE

Suddenly, Grant saved the day!

"Hey, Mimi and Papa, can we go next door to the bookstore while you guys finish your food? And I just saw that Lawyer Tradd guy come in. Maybe you have some new questions for him?" Grant pointed to a nearby table.

Mimi was always in favor of kids in a bookstore. "Sure," she said. "If you go right next door then come right back."

Papa handed them each a ten dollar bill. "Buy a book," he said.

"Thanks!" both kids squealed, then hopped up and dashed out before their grandparents could think twice and change their minds. It wasn't like them to turn them loose so easily, but they could see the bookstore, and besides, Mimi knew the owner and would probably call on her cell phone and request "surveillance" on her grandkids!

Quickly, the two kids headed toward the door. Suddenly, Christina ran back to the table and grabbed her coat and Grant's hat. Mimi smiled, and Christina knew she thought they were dressing for the weather, but that was not the case at all.

When Christina met her brother at the door, she slammed his hat on his head and tugged the bill low over his eyes. She pulled on her trench coat, belted it tightly, and yanked the collar up around her face.

"What's this all about?" Grant asked, as they dashed next door to the Blue Bicycle Bookstore.

"We're incognito," whispered Christina.

"We're in big trouble is what we are," said Grant, "if we look too suspicious. Mimi's still watching us, you know." Together the kids gave their grandparents a wave and a grin.

But as soon as they turned away, they were all serious.

In a few moments, they were able to slip into the bookstore. There were just a few customers. The clerk nodded politely, then went back to her work.

"You scout around for Ashley and Cooper," Christina whispered to Grant. "I have a quick errand to run." As soon as she said this, Christina headed toward another part of the store.

Grant shrugged his shoulders and decided to head for the kids' book section. It was not long before he had forgotten what they had come for. He found a good mystery, sat on the floor, yanked off his cap and started to read, soon lost in an exciting story.

In the meantime, Christina was in the Local Books section, reading up on the Civil War, especially its beginning at Fort Sumter. Soon, she too, was lost in the fascinating history of that era.

So it was not surprising when both kids simultaneously looked up and found Ashley staring at Grant and Cooper frowning at Christina. When Christina and Grant looked up in shock, both girls said, "Come with us!"

In just a moment, the four kids gathered in a back corner of the store.

"Grant!" said Christina, "you were supposed to be the lookout!"

Her brother frowned. "Sorry, I got to reading..."

Ashley and Cooper giggled. "Don't worry, about it," Ashley said. "We've been watching for you out the window."

"But why?" asked Christina, puzzled. "We thought you were hiding from us."

Cooper sighed. "Well, we were. But then, uh, then we decided we needed your help."

"Our help?" said Grant. "I think we need your help. You live here, after all. We're strangers in these parts." He did his best lost cowboy look, like Papa did sometimes when he was in trouble with Mimi.

Christina was suspicious. "Help with what?" she asked.

Ashley shrugged. "We aren't exactly allowed to say," she said.

Cooper nodded in agreement.

"Then how can we help you and why do you think we can, anyway?" asked Grant.

Now Cooper frowned. "Well, what do you need our help for, anyway?" she retorted.

It was easy for the four kids to see that they were at an impasse. They each realized that they would have to share some TOP SECRET information to make any headway in their individual mysteries. As they sat on the floor and discussed the matter, they realized that they were each involved in the same mystery—and each in a lot of trouble!

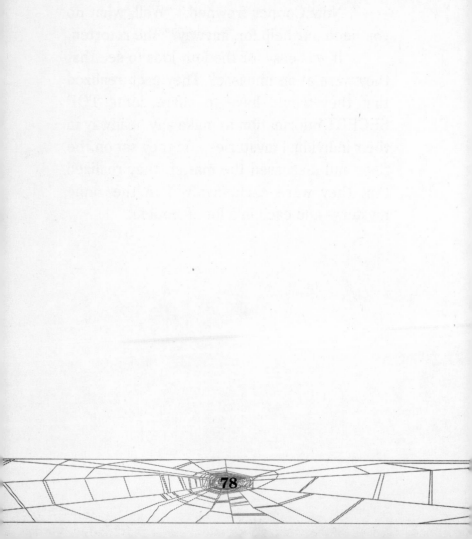

10

THE SUM(TER) OF ALL FEARS

"So let me get this straight," said Christina. "You girls want us to help you find out who is stealing historic artifacts from Fort Sumter, but you can't tell us why, right?"

Ashley and Cooper nodded eagerly.

"And you want us to help you figure out who is sending you clues regarding the theft of cannonballs and other historic stuff from around Charleston, correct?" asked Ashley.

Christina and Grant nodded.

"But we can tell you why," said Grant. "People often try to get our grandmother in hot water when she's around, being a mystery book writer and all. It's the only explanation for us to be getting these clues that, well, that don't mean anything to us."

"We just want to solve the mystery of the missing cannonballs so we can get back home to Peachtree City in time for Christmas," added Christina sadly.

"Well, we also have to figure out the mystery of the missing Au..." Grant began, when suddenly, Christina slapped her hand across his mouth.

"Uh, Grant," she said urgently. "Let's not burden our new friends with all our problems!" she warned and managed to give him a private wink.

"Uh, sure, sis," said Grant, rubbing his mouth. "But how do we know these girls are our friends?"

Ashley and Cooper looked hurt.

"We need your help because we read your grandmother's books. We know you two help her solve mysteries. Gee, we thought you'd be eager to help," said Ashley.

"And right away!" added Cooper with a desperate look.

Just as Christina was about to grill them about what the rush was, they all were surprised when Ashley and Cooper's mother turned the corner and almost fell over them.

"My, goodness!" she said, sounding more amused than aggravated. "What in the world are you kids doing sitting on the floor in the dark back here?" She looked down at the book Christina was holding. "Hmm," she said in a surprised, perhaps even suspicious voice, "interested in Fort Sumter, are you?"

In spite of themselves, both Christina and Grant gave her a 'guilty as charged' look. "I, uh, that is..." Christina began. But the woman ignored her.

"Come on, girls," their mom said. "Say goodbye and meet me at the register. I have to get back to work, you know." Then she turned on her heel and paraded toward the front of the store.

It was one of those times where you have to make a quick decision.

"Look," said Christina. "Here are the clues we've gotten so far. If they mean something to you, call us on this cell phone number." She scribbled Mimi's extra cell phone number on a bookmark. Her grandmother always gave her and Grant a phone to use when they were traveling, just in case they got separated, which happened more than anyone would ever imagine!

Ashley took the clues and the bookmark and nodded. "We will!" she promised.

Cooper looked at her sister oddly. "But we don't need the clu..." she began.

Just as Christina had done, Cooper slapped her hand over her sister's mouth with a nervous giggle. "Don't worry about it, sis," she said, standing and tugging her sister up. "Come on! Mom's waiting." As she tugged her sister up the aisle, she added, "We'll be in touch, I promise!"

When they vanished, Grant asked his sister, "Well, what was that all about?"

Christina shook her head. "Who knows?"

Then she and Grant froze as they peered over the edge of the plate glass window. Passing by, staring into the foggy window, was the bellman, yet again. And right behind him, arm in arm, and innocently happy, were their grandparents. They passed by and headed into the bookstore.

"We either have too much help or no help solving this mystery," Grant moaned.

Christina sighed and stood up. "What we have is no time. Christmas is just a couple of days away." Grant was shocked to see a tear form in his sister's eye. But, of course, he felt like crying himself.

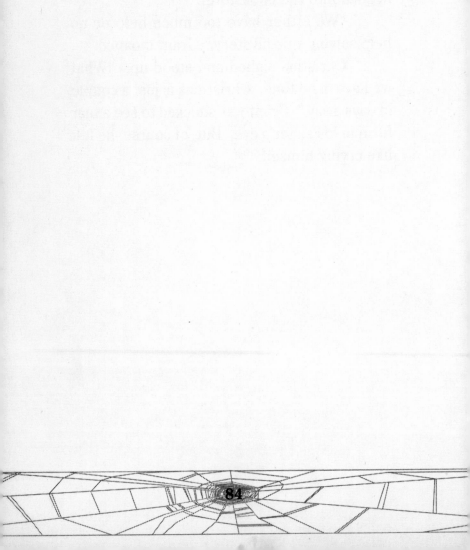

11

A KING OF A STREET

As soon as Mimi and Papa came in the store, Grant and Christina appeared at the checkout desk with their books.

Mimi peeked at the historic title Christina had selected and nodded approvingly. Then she looked at the book Grant held. "Grant!" she said, "that's one of my books. You can have all my books you want, silly boy, what's up?"

"Just thought I'd help get you on the bestseller list," Grant said shyly. Mimi beamed her appreciation, but shook her head, and sent Papa and Grant back to the kids' section to swap it for another book.

"What am I going to do with that sweet grandson of mine?" Mimi asked Christina.

Christina shook her head. "What to do with Grant is a constant question of mine, Mimi," she said with a giggle and her grandmother frowned.

"Well, I'm glad to see you're interested in local Charleston history," Mimi said, "but I didn't know you were so interested in the Civil War."

As she waited for her change, Christina said, "I think I might have a report to do on the Civil War this year. Just thought I'd prepare ahead of time."

Her grandmother nodded in understanding. When Grant and Papa reappeared with a different book, Christina turned in time to see Ashley, Cooper, and their mother hurrying down the street, as the bellman passed them on his silly bike with the silly bell.

Back at the hotel, they waited on a call from Lawyer Tradd. Mimi napped and Papa watched a football game in the bedroom. In the living room, Christina and Grant camped out with their books, hot chocolate, and chocolate chip cookies.

Grant seemed to have forgotten about their mystery woes and chores, but Christina felt a real sense of urgency as she read her book. She really didn't know much about the so-called War Between the States but soon found herself very interested.

"Hey, Grant, listen to this," she said, poking her sleepy brother in his side with her bare toe.

"At this time in America's history, slaves were used in the South to farm crops and do chores. Abolitionists (people opposed to slavery) wanted President Lincoln to make slavery illegal. Other people argued over the issue of whether individual states or the federal government should decide such matters.

"There was such a big disagreement that on December 20, 1860, South Carolina seceded (withdrew) from the Union. Soon, other states left the Union and created the Confederate States of America. This meant that the United States was now virtually two different countries, each angry and fearful of the other.

"Fort Sumter was a U.S. fort in Charleston Harbor. Confederate soldiers from South Carolina demanded that Union soldiers surrender the fort. On April 12, 1861, the Confederates bombarded Fort Sumter with their cannons. People from Charleston climbed onto the roofs of their homes to watch the 34-hour show of firepower.

"This was the 'first shot fired in the Civil War' and although Fort Sumter surrendered and no one was killed, it was the beginning of a terrible war that lasted four years, killed more than half a million soldiers, and left America in devastation for many years even after the war, during the long, hard era known as Reconstruction."

Grant only wanted to know one thing: "Well, who won?"

"The Yankees!" said Christina with a frown.

"So we were the Yankees?" asked Grant, excitedly.

"No, Grant!" said his sister. "We live in the South. We were the Confederates. We lost!"

Just then Papa entered the room. He plopped down in one of the armchairs and rubbed his face. "Actually, kids," he said, "no one truly won that war. President Lincoln's Emancipation Proclamation freed the slaves, which was good, but it was not a pretty picture for anyone."

"What do you mean?" asked Grant, confused. He loved video games and thought winning was winning and losing was losing.

"Well," said Papa, "do you think if we had a battle in our family with one side against the other, that would be good?"

"No," both kids answered, eager to see what their grandfather, who loved history, was getting at.

Papa sighed. "When Americans fought Americans in that war, it was not good either. We didn't have a Revolutionary War to get our nation, just to divide it in half. On the battlefield, it was often brother fighting against brother. The war was cruel. Weapons killed and made brutal wounds. Like Grant told us at the fort, if you didn't die, you often had an arm, or leg, or both amputated! And there was no anesthesia, except maybe a stick between your teeth to bite down on, or a swig of whiskey. Homes were burned, cities were burned, people went hungry, lost all they had, and even the freed slaves were often at a loss over what to do next. Even though slavery was 100% wrong, it was all many of them had known."

For a moment both children were very quiet.

"What happened next?" Christina finally asked, a little afraid to hear the answer.

"After the war, everyone tried to pick up the pieces of their lives," said Papa. "But Reconstruction was just about as hard as the war. Most folks didn't have any pieces to pick up. As is often the case, some bad people tried to take advantage of the situation. Carpetbaggers and scalawags, they were called."

"Were they like robbers?" Grant asked, now not so excited about the idea of war.

"Robbers, looters, and worse!" swore Papa.

With a careful glance at his sister, Grant changed the subject. "So, uh, Papa, what are cannons?"

Papa gave his grandson a puzzled look. "You know," he said. "Those big, black guns you see mounted at forts to **defend** it."

"And cannonballs?" Grant added.

Papa still looked puzzled. "Uh, those black iron balls you see stacked up beside the cannons. The soldiers stuff them and gunpowder in the cannon. They light a fuse and cry, 'FIRE IN THE HOLE!' so everyone knows to stand clear, then there's a giant KABOOM!"

"So they're just old guns?" asked Christina, having figured out what Grant was asking about.

Papa rubbed his face again and stood up. "No, where they still exist at forts and in museums, they are valuable artifacts. They are historic. HISTORY!" Papa stalked off to the bathroom to shave.

It was a good thing because just then the cell phone in Christina's pocket rang. She grabbed for it and answered in a whisper, "Hello?"

12

A CALL FROM THE DEAD

When there was no answer, Christina repeated, "Hello? Hello?"

Finally, a small, squeaky voice answered on the other end. "Christina, is that you?"

"Yes, ma'am," Christina said, surprised that she was not talking to Ashley or Cooper. She had no idea who this could be except a call for Mimi or a wrong number.

"Well, this is Lulu!" the woman said. Christina fell back onto the sofa cushions in shock.

"But, Aunt Lulu," she finally managed to squeak out herself. "You're, uh, you're dead!"

Grant stared at his sister; his mouth fell open and he hopped up to try to listen to the phone too, but his sister pushed him away.

Aunt Lulu cackled, her voice stronger now. "That's what they hoped to convince everyone!" she said.

"Who?" asked Christina. Her hand quivered as she grasped the phone to her ear. She did not understand.

"Why, the carpetbaggers and the scalawags, that's who!" said Aunt Lulu. "It's a conspiracy, I'll tell you that! They won't get away with their dastardly shenanigans! You and your brother meet me in ten minutes at the Museum of Charleston. I'm wearing a long white dress and a big, floppy white hat. You won't miss me!" And before Christina could answer, Aunt Lulu hung up.

"WHAT? WHAT?" wailed Grant, when Christina closed the phone and shoved it in her pocket.

Christina just hopped up and peeked in the bedroom. Mimi was sound asleep. She could hear Papa's portable razor humming in the bathroom. Quickly, she grabbed the notepad by the desk phone, scribbled on it, and ran for the door.

"Come on, Grant! We have to go, right now!"

Grant hopped up and followed his sister, who let the door close silently behind them. She had forgotten to bring a key. "Where are we going?" he asked as they ran down the hall. "What are we going to do?"

Christina turned, and wide-eyed, called back to him as they raced to the lobby, "Find carpetbaggers and scalawags...and, and, Aunt Lulu!"

Grant was bug-eyed. "War!" he cried. "IT'S WAR!"

Fortunately, Christina had spotted the Museum of Charleston very near the hotel. They scampered down Bay Street, wishing they had grabbed their coats. As soon as they got to the museum, they looked all around for a woman in a white dress and hat; none was to be seen.

Since they hadn't brought any money, either, they couldn't get a ticket to get inside the museum. They both felt very frustrated. If only Aunt Lulu would spy them and show herself!

Suddenly, Grant shoved his sister behind a brick post.

"What is it?" Christina demanded, aggravated.

"Him!" Grant hissed, pointing.

The bellman on the bike was following them again. From the look on his face, he clearly feared he had lost them, which made both kids smile. He didn't even ring his tinny little bell, just paused with one foot on a pedal, staring at all four corners, wondering which way to go.

As usual, Grant surprised his sister by suddenly darting out from behind the post and accosting the bellman. "Who are you?!" he demanded. "And why are you following us, you, you, you scalawag!"

Shocked, the bellman almost fell off his bike. He looked even more nervous when

Christina ran forward and joined her brother. The young man put up both his hands. "It's ok! I promise! Guilty as charged! I have been following you."

"But why?" Christina pleaded.

"Your grandfather asked me to," said the bellman with a gentle grin. "He said you kids often walk about and he just wanted to be sure you were ok." He frowned. "I guess you are, but you sure are a handful to keep up with."

Suddenly, Christina looked startled. "You mean Papa knows where we are?"

The bellman shook his head. "No. I just spotted you race out of the hotel and I was on my lunch break, so I decided to follow you and see what was up. What are you kids always racing around about—it's sort of weird, you know."

Grant just grinned, but his sister sighed. "It's a long story," she said, wearily. Then she decided the bellman was harmless and maybe could help them. "We're looking for our Aunt Lulu, white dress, white hat."

"DEAD..." Grant interrupted.

The young man looked startled.

"NOT!" Christina promised. "But do you know anything about a local black market, I'd guess you'd call it, for stolen historic artifacts, by chance?" she tried to ask nonchalantly.

The bellman looked worried and threw up his hands. "Uh, I don't know what you kids are involved in but I don't want any part of..."

Christina started to interrupt him to explain, when Grant shocked them both by grabbing the bell and ringing it like crazy.

"What is it, Grant?" Christina asked.

Her brother pointed down the street. "AUNT LULU ALERT!" he said. "She's headed toward Meeting Street—let's roll!"

The bellman shook his head. "Uh, I think I'm the only one who can roll. You guys follow me and I'll go ahead and see if I can find her."

Before they could answer, he biked off. That made Christina nervous. He could reach Aunt Lulu first, and she still was not sure whether he was a good guy, or one of those carpetbagger/scalawag types. But for now it didn't matter. Grant had raced off down the street and all she could do was run after him...as fast as she could!

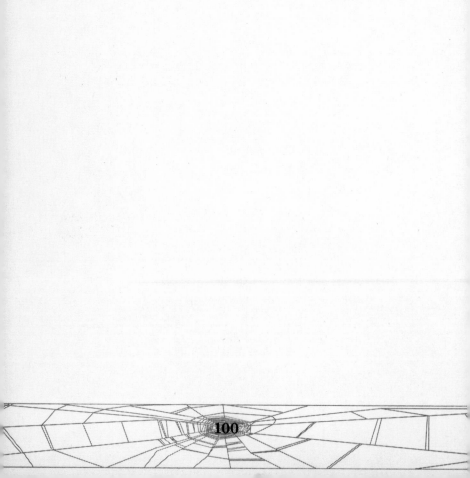

13

IT'S OUR CUSTOM...

Charleston is an extraordinary town. In addition to being as steeped in history as hot tea bags...being drop dead gorgeous...and having some of the most delicious food in the nation, it's also some other things:

• Confusing: A snarl of waterways, bridges, streets, roads, and unusual names such as The Battery, make it very challenging for visitors to get around, but very easy for them to get LOST!

• Busy!: Downtown Charleston is a bustling city any time of the year, filled with residents, workers, government officials, nautical types, college students, medical personnel (hospitals), tourists, tourists, tourists, and traffic, traffic, traffic—well, things can get confusing and folks can get LOST!

• Mesmerizing: You can be strolling in one direction, absolutely sure where you are going, when suddenly you spy a gorgeous historic home that you just have to walk around an entire block to see all of...or a shop chock full of wonderful things that you just must pop inside to see...or a curious individual who looks like they might have walked right out of the past, so you follow them—just a little ways, to see what's up—and next thing you know: Yep, you're LOST!

On the cold, winter's day of December 22, LOST happened to the entire party of Mimi, Papa, Christina, Grant, and, well, most everyone else. At first it was just a little disconcerting. Soon, it was quite nerve-wracking. And later, it was totally panicsville. The afternoon went something like this:

CHRISTINA: *"Grant, you follow the bellman to Meeting Street. I'll hurry on down Bay and see if I spy Aunt Lulu. Meet me at the Old Slave Market!"*

GRANT: *"OK! I'll run down King Street, and you check over on that side of downtown, and we'll meet in front of S.N.O.B."*

BELLMAN: *"She went right, she went right! Follow me!"* *[Grant goes left; Christina goes straight.]*

MIMI: *"Where are our grandkids?!"* *[Since she can't find Papa and he has the note Christina left, she runs out to go to Lawyer Tradd's office.]*

PAPA: *"Have you seen my grandchildren? Or the bellman I've been talking to?"* *[No one has, so Papa leaves the hotel in search of them. He goes left; Mimi, a few minutes behind him, turns right.]*

ASHLEY: *"Christina? I'm so glad you answered your cell phone. I think we have info.*

Please meet us at the Blue Bicycle bookstore. It's on King. Ok? Good, see you there in five minutes!" [Ashley heads toward the bookstore; Christina thinks she said Queen Street and heads there.]

COOPER: *"Ashley! I think I just saw Grant go by! I'm going to go find him and bring him to the bookstore, ok?" [She does not wait for her sister to answer; she runs down Meeting Street, but does not see that Grant has turned into an alley and passes right by him.]*

MOTHER: *"Ashley? Cooper? Where are you girls? Oh, dear, I left my notebook! Stay where you are—I'll be right back!"*

LAWYER TRADD: *"I'm going home for a lunch and a nap. If that Carole Marsh woman comes by, tell her I'll see her tomorrow...maybe. I have no idea where her aunt is!"*

AUNT LULU: *"Help! Help! Isn't anyone going to come find me?"*

14

THE SWAMPFOX

His name is John Dalton, like one of the Dalton Gang from outlaw days. His alias is Johnny Dee. He has almost completed his Big Giant Plan! For thirty days, he has been stealing historic artifacts from historic sites in Charleston. It is almost for certain that no one is on to him!

Oh, yes, there have been articles in the *Charleston Post and Courier*. And Letters to the Editor complaining about no one finding the "Cannonball Thief" as he has been nicknamed. He likes that! And an editorial about how national parks and monuments lack the funds to guard the nation's treasures as adequately as they would like to. And a funny political cartoon of a thief who looks an awful lot like him walking right down King Street juggling half a dozen black cannonballs. The caption read: Is Fort Sumter under attack again?!

And then there was the paid obituary for one Lulu Anna Thurmond, age 90, deceased, Charleston born and bred.

"Lazy Lawyer Tradd's just about that old," the Swampfox mused to himself. "Maybe his obituary will be next?"

The Swampfox, as he had nicknamed himself, was busy piling the many cannonballs and other artifacts he had stolen into a special container. His ruse was perfect, he thought! And he was almost done here in Charleston and could move on and tackle another historic area rich in artifacts. He felt confident and happy. Indeed, invincible. All the things that can set someone up for failure?

John Dalton slammed the lid of the convenient "container," nailed it shut, and put a big, fat, official shipping label on it. As soon as Fed Ex picked it up, it would head to his brother Jim Dalton, alias Rex Tondal, out in Phoenix. First flight out, and boy would they have a high old time, just in time for a very, merry Christmas! "I mean what could go wrong now?" the smarmy Swampfox muttered to himself.

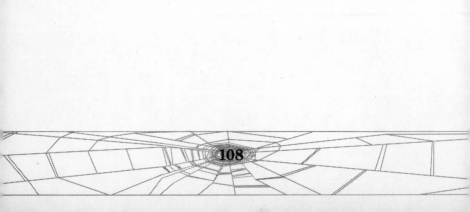

15

THE FOG COMES ON LITTLE FAT FEET

It was December 22 and they should have headed for home already, Christina thought. Mimi should be home baking yummy cakes for Christmas. Her mom would be busy trying to close the Gallopade publishing offices for the holidays. Her dad and Papa would still be buying last minute gifts and rearranging Christmas lights. Uncle Michael would be listening to the ever-longer Christmas list that Avery and Ella would be writing while Aunt Cassidy baked cookies for Santa. Evan would be revving up for his first Christmas as a walker, which would be so much fun to watch. She and Grant would be playing with friends, shaking packages beneath the tree, and anxiously awaiting the Big Day. She had never "missed" Christmas, and Christina could not imagine doing so this year. But it was clear that was probably what would happen. She was just about to cry.

To make things worse, the afternoon was fading away. A cotton ball layer of clouds hung low over the city and it had begun to snow again. It was getting dark so early these days, especially down here on the East Coast. And, worst of all, she could not find Grant. Truly, Christina did not know what to do.

She climbed the slick steps of the enormous, white marble Custom House. She thought perhaps she might spy Grant if she got up high enough. But in the fog and snow, all she could see—and barely that—was the beautiful blue South Carolina flag with its white quarter moon and palmetto tree. It whipped in the wind like a blue blur.

Christina knew she should go back to the hotel and tell her grandparents what was going on. It was the only responsible thing to do. But she and Grant had never given up on a mystery before. Besides, she knew she would be in Big Trouble if she returned alone and admitted that she had lost her brother!

Lost. All seemed so lost.

Grant was exhausted. He just couldn't chase the bicycle fast enough to keep up. He knew he was totally lost. What should he do now, he wondered. He tried to think of what his sister would do. She was really good at solving mysteries, but he couldn't solve this mystery all alone, and all alone is exactly what he was right now. It was getting colder by the minute. He was lonesome and scared. He knew Mimi and Papa would croak when they found out he and Christina had not stayed together. But suddenly, he saw ahead in the swirling fog big M and U and S letters and believed that he was back at the Charleston

Museum where they had started. Maybe if he stood here, his sister would show up? So that is what he did. Only Grant was not standing in front of the Charleston Museum. He was standing in front of the Children's Museum of Charleston. And no one was looking for him there.

Ashley wondered why in the world she had run off without her sister. How foolish was that? They had been staying at an inn downtown, but now, not only could she not find it, she could not even remember its name. So even if she asked an adult for help, what would she say: "I'm lost." What good would that do? She had never seen Grant, or anyone, for that matter, and now, in the ever-increasing snow, she couldn't see much at all. And it was cold! What to do? She sat on a cold step to think about it, but nothing came to her.

Mimi was beside herself! It was one thing to lose dead Aunt Lulu. But it was another for her entire family to go missing—without a word or a note or a phone call! She had tried Christina's cell phone, but it was either dead or turned off. She just hoped their parents did not call and she had to admit that she had lost their children, and right here at Christmas too! And where was Papa? It was not like her husband to run off and leave her at all. What in the world was going on? And it was so cold and she had left her gloves back in the room. Mimi spied a Saks Fifth Avenue and ran inside. She sped to a counter heaped in colorful gloves and mittens. As she was making her purchase, the contents of her purse spilled out onto the floor. When she bent down to retrieve them, she came face-to-face with a smiling Santa Claus!

"Can I help you?" he asked kindly. "What is your Christmas wish?"

All but in tears, Mimi quickly thrust the scattered items back into her purse, with Santa's help.

"Oh, my wish list is too long this year, Santa," she said, "and it can't wait till Christmas. Thanks, anyway, but I really have to run. Merry Christmas, though," she added, and grabbed her sack and dashed out into the street.

"I'm really in big trouble when even Santa can't help me!" Mimi muttered to herself. She had no idea where to go, but she had a hunch, so she turned left and hurried up King Street as fast as the slick sidewalk would allow.

Papa drummed his fingers so loudly on the countertop that the waiter asked, "Are you alright, sir? Is there a problem with the service?"

"No, no," Papa said. "The service is fine. I'm just waiting for someone, only I'm not sure they are coming." He looked very sad and concerned, his usually merry face a crisscross of worry.

"A young lady?" the waiter inquired, clearly trying to help, not be nosy.

Papa sighed. "A young lady, an old lady, I'll take any lady who comes along!" Quickly Papa corrected himself with a blush. "What I mean is my wife is missing, and my granddaughter, and my grandson."

"Perhaps all shopping?" the waiter guessed. "'Tis the season..."

"The season for trouble!" Papa said. "I think I'll just wait and watch out this window, if you don't mind. I've looked everywhere and all I can think is that maybe they will come back to the hotel soon. It's going to be dark soon and the snow is really picking up."

The waiter nodded and wiped his hands on his apron. "Very unusual weather for

Charleston," he agreed. "And supposed to get worse. I would not want to be out in this tonight." He turned and went back to his work.

Papa just looked more worried than ever and drummed his fingers louder— PA RUM PA PUM PUM!

Cooper looked at her watch. Her mom was going to be so upset! How could she let Ashley get away from her? And what was the name of that inn they were staying in, anyway? Had her mom gone back to Fort Sumter? Surely not in this weather? To the police? Her mother had been up late last night on the computer and this morning said she had a hunch about somebody named the Swampfox, but that meant nothing to Cooper. She was freezing cold and the snow was sticking to her eyelashes, but she couldn't see much anyway for the gloom. Still, she had one idea, so she snugged her hands under her arms and trudged on.

Ashley and Cooper's mother was perturbed. She couldn't find her girls and could only suppose, and hope, that they had returned to the inn. As the type of national park employee that she was, she was used to spending a lot of time alone, but she felt especially alone this late, winter afternoon. It was busier, but cheerier, when the girls were around. And she was now worried, with the weather, if they would be able to make it to her own mother's house in Columbia in time for the holidays. It was a true "joke" that when it snowed in the South, no one knew how to drive—but they got out and tried anyway. What a mess! She looked over her notes from the Fort Sumter tour and thought hard. Suddenly, she snapped her fingers, tossed her cold coffee into a nearby trashcan, and scooted off down the street in a big hurry. She could only hope her hunch was right!

The bellman gave up. He had been up and down every downtown street for the last hour and never seen the kids or Aunt Lulu. He hated to let the nice grandpa down, but really, there was only so much he could do to chase after a couple of kids who did not seem to want to be caught up with. And this Aunt Lulu business worried him. He did not want to inadvertently be an accomplice to some crime, or something. He was just a lowly bellman after some extra tips so he could buy his girlfriend an engagement ring and make her his fiancé for Christmas. Was that too much to ask? Dejectedly, he said aloud to the spiraling snow, "I guess it is." Then he turned the bike around and skidded his way back toward the hotel and his next shift.

Aunt Lulu snored softly. She thought the people here were very nice, maybe too nice. They were so protective that they would not even let her leave the cozy, little upstairs room over the Tradd Law Firm. She was old, but she was not senile, and she had some Christmas shopping to do. She listened carefully and when she heard only the silence of falling snow decided that everyone down below had gone home for the day. She began to get dressed. She would Christmas shop. She would!

16

A SNOW SLAP IN THE FACE

The cell phone startled Christina almost out of her frozen skin when it rang. Her cold fingers fumbled it open. "Hello?" she wheezed. "Who is this?"

A voice on the other end of the line gasped. "It's your Mimi, that's who! Where in the world are you?"

Christina coughed and stretched. She believed that she had actually fallen asleep on the icy steps. It was almost dark!

"I'm on the steps of the U.S. Custom House," she told her grandmother.

"Well, stay right there! I'm on my way to pick you up. I've had a call about Lulu. The lawyer swears they've found her!"

Christina was shocked but disappointed when her grandmother hung up. Still, she was thrilled to think that Aunt Lulu had been found, and wondered for sure if she was alive—or not?!—and where she had been all this time. She could hardly wait for her grandmother to show up and rescue her!

17
SNOW BIKE

Papa peered through the frosty glass and saw the bellman coming. "He's back!" he said aloud and dashed from his table to greet the boy at the door.

"Did you find them?" he asked urgently, before the boy could even climb off his bike. The bellman looked exhausted. He plucked the $20 bill from his pocket and thrust it at Papa.

"I'm real sorry, sir," he said, with the sorrow of failure in his voice. "I tried, I really did, but those kids..."

"I know, I know!" Papa said, nodding his head up and down. "But where did you see them last?"

The boy thought back through the last hours. "Grant was following me down Meeting Street. I was chasing after Aunt Lulu."

"Aunt Lulu?!" squealed Papa. "Why, she's...Oh, never mind!" he interrupted himself. "Let me borrow your bike," he added but it was not a request. Before the bellman could object, Papa hopped on the bicycle and sped off down the driveway.

He had not gone far at all when he found his grandson pathetically trudging down a side street. With a spewing skiff of snow, Papa screeched to a halt.

"Papa!" cried Grant. "I'm so glad to see you! I waited and waited at the museum but I think it was the wrong one. I'm cold and lost and scared and I have no idea where Christina is and I know you and Mimi are mad and worried and Aunt Lulu must be frozen to death by now in that thin old white dress and..."

Papa grabbed his grandson in a bear hug. "It's ok, Grant," he assured him, rubbing his hands up and down Grant's arms to warm him up. "I have no idea what you are talking about, but everything will be fine, I promise." Grant looked up at his grandfather with tears in his eyes. "No, Papa, I don't think it will be," he said sadly.

Papa just plucked his grandson up off the sidewalk and stuffed his little bottom into the straw basket on the front of the bike. "It will too!" he promised. "You just ring this little bell so folks will hear we are coming in this snowstorm. You'll see."

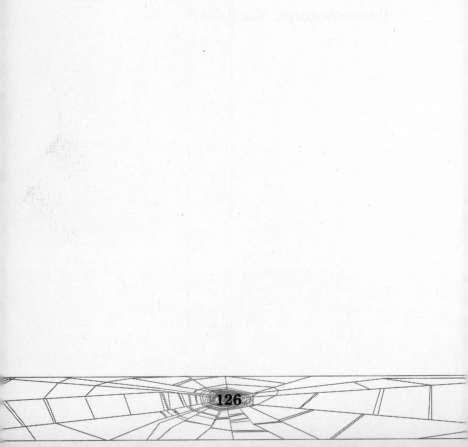

I'm freeeeezzzzing!

18

BLOCKADE!

Ashley and Cooper's mother pulled up in front of the bookstore and, just as she had suspected, saw her bedraggled daughters sitting on stools staring out two frosty holes they had whittled in the foggy window.

"MOM?!" she saw them mouth. They waved happily and hopped off the stools and ran out to her car. They could hardly wait to climb in the warm backseat.

"We are sooooooooooo glad to see you!" cried Cooper.

"Please don't be mad!" begged Ashley. "We can explain!"

Their mother just stared ahead and sped down the road and around the corner.

"There's no time for that now," she told her girls. "But later!" she warned. "I might have this thing figured out, maybe, anyway. I hope so."

"And we can go to grandma's?" the girls asked eagerly.

Their mother did not answer. Adroitly, she parallel parked in front of the Tradd Law Firm. She got out of the car and motioned for the girls to follow.

19

UNDER SIEGE!

It was a crazy scene. It looked as if the tiny law office was under attack by an assortment of cold and weary defendants, eager to have their say in court.

Miss Lonesome, the secretary to Lawyer Tradd, was shocked when Mimi, Papa, another woman, and a passel of kids pounded up the steps and into the room, bringing a flurry of slinging snow inside with them.

"What's going on?" she demanded. "I am just about to lock up and leave! You have no right to be here! Mr. Tradd is out for the holidays."

"NO, I'M NOT!" the elderly lawyer shouted as he made his own way up the steps, using his cane to keep from sliding. Papa helped him inside. "You called me?" he turned to Mimi and said.

"No," said Mimi. "YOU called me. You said Aunt Lulu had been found!"

The lawyer looked puzzled, and embarrassed. "Yes," he admitted. "I think I did. I mean I might have. I forget. I went home to take a nap. Miss Lonesome said I did not feel good."

Mimi looked at the woman in the national park uniform. "And who would you be?" she asked.

Grant piped up merrily. "Oh, that's Ashley and Cooper's mom!" he said, as if that explained everything.

"Who?" asked Mimi, but when she looked at the girls she remembered. "Yes, you were at Fort Sumter that day, and in the café, and in the bookstore—my goodness, what is going on?"

"Not goodness, that's for sure!" said the woman. "I'm Agent Moo and I am a private eye, I mean detective, for the National Park

Service. I've been investigating the theft of all the historic artifacts from Fort Sumter and around Charleston this past month."

Papa looked perplexed. "But what does that have to do with us?" he demanded. "Or this law firm? Or Aunt Lulu? Rest her soul." Then he added in a booming voice, "GRAAAAANT?"

"No, not me!" said Grant. "I didn't take anything. Really."

"I'm not sure," Agent Moo interrupted. She pulled out her notepad. "But my daughters found, or were given, some clues that seem to have been directed to your grandchildren..."

"Famous for butting into mysteries they have nothing to do with," Mimi said with a frown.

Agent Moo nodded. She frowned at her own children. "I know exactly what you mean," she said. "But each clue had a little bit of a letterhead on it. When my girls disappeared today, I found these clues and put the pieces together until I could read the business' name: this law firm!"

Lawyer Tradd looked astounded. "But I am on the board of the historical society!" He seemed appalled to think that someone thought he could be a thief.

Mimi and Agent Moo exchanged glances.

"Perhaps you are not who Agent Moo has in mind," Mimi suggested. She stared at Miss Lonesome, who looked very nervous.

"How long has Miss Lonesome worked for you?" Agent Moo asked Lawyer Tradd.

The man looked very disoriented. "Why, I'm not sure! Not long, I don't think. I seem to be so addled these days, I'm sorry. Oh, yes, I think about thirty days?"

Miss Lonesome grew quite pale and made a sudden dash for another door in the office. It would not open. "Open it!" she screamed. "Open it now!"

Everyone stared, mouths agape, as the door flew open and a man in a white dress and a white hat, but wearing big, black boots, stood before them. Behind him was a coffin. He had a hammer in his hand and it was clear that he was nailing it shut!

"Stand back!" shouted Agent Moo.

Papa moved to protect the children. Mimi looked like she might faint. Lawyer Tradd fell backwards into an armchair.

"Ok, Swampfox, get us out of this mess!" Miss Lonesome demanded hatefully. "I'm sorry I ever got hooked up with you, you loser!"

John Dalton looked too shocked to speak or move. He could easily see that Agent Moo wore a gun on her hip. "Ok, ok!" he whimpered. "Guess I know where I'm spending Christmas." He tossed the hammer down.

From upstairs there was a large thud. Everyone stared upward.

"And just what was THAT?!" boomed Papa.

In a tiny voice, Grant guessed, "Santa?"

20

OH WHAT FUN IT IS...

Agent Moo stood in front of John Dalton and Miss Lonesome while Papa climbed a tiny set of stairs to a small door.

"It's just storage," Lawyer Tradd said from his chair, but no one listened to him.

Carefully, Papa tugged the door open a crack. He found himself face to face with Aunt Lulu!

It was hard to say who looked more surprised. In fact, everyone was SHOCKED, except John Dalton and Miss Lonesome.

"You're not dead?" Papa said gently.

To their further surprise, tiny Aunt Lulu, also in a white dress and a white hat, tapped Papa on the chest. "Why, of course not, young man! If I were, I think I would know it. Now move out of my way. I'm going Christmas shopping!" She shoved her way past Papa.

But suddenly, the old woman looked faint. "Carole?" she said. Tears arose in her faded blue eyes. "Is that you, honey child?"

Mimi burst into tears and ran to catch her Aunt Lulu before she pelted down the stairs.

In the meantime, Agent Moo had called the local police and a blue light now turned the snow outside into a strange color. They entered the building and headed to where Agent Moo pointed.

"But where's the booty?" asked one of the cops, as if they had just busted a buccaneer.

"Check the coffin," Agent Moo suggested.

"Uh, negatory on that, I think!" said the second officer.

"Oh, for heaven's sake!" said Christina and dashed forward.

Before the adults could stop her or the other kids, they grabbed the hammer and began to tug on the lid of the cheap wooden box. As the top popped off, everyone gasped. Inside was a heaping pile of cannonballs and other historic artifacts.

Papa leaned over and read the shipping label: "PHOENIX, ARIZONA. You almost got away with it, buddy."

Suddenly all the kids burst out laughing.

"Why, what in the world can be so funny at a time like this?" asked Mimi, who was both smiling with relief over Aunt Lulu being alive, and crumbling with dismay at all that was happening.

Grant wiped his nose on his sleeve. "Well, for one thing," he said, pointing to the miserable John Dalton, "what kind of respectable crook wears an old lady dress...and combat boots?" The girls giggled.

"And how did you think you were going to get this shipped Fed Ex anyway?" asked Christina with a smug smile. "It's way overweight for any domestic shipment."

"How did you know that, kid?" John Dalton demanded, as he was handcuffed.

"I help in a publishing company," Christina answered smugly. "In the shipping department."

Suddenly, Mimi began to bawl! LOUDLY! Very loudly!

"Oh, dear!" said Papa. "What in the world is wrong now?!"

21

IT'S BEGINNING TO LOOK A LOT LIKE YOU KNOW WHAT!

"IT'S MY BIRTHDAY!" Mimi wailed. Papa burst out laughing. "But you don't look your age, woman!" he said.

"But we forgot it, Papa!" said Grant.

"Is that what's wrong, Mimi?" Christina begged her grandmother. "We're sorry! We can make it up to you. We never forget your birthday, even if it is so close to Christmas."

"No, no," said Mimi, drying her tears. "It's not that. It's that it is almost Christmas and...and...we are all here...and BOO HOO BOO!!!...they are all there!"

Now, all the women were crying and the kids too, all of them.

"They?" asked Lawyer Tradd. "They who?"

"US!" said Uncle Michael, as he opened the office door. "The rest of the family. We never miss Mimi's birthday, do we Mimi?"

Mimi beamed as Uncle Michael, Aunt Cassidy, Avery, 7, Ella, 5, and Evan, the toddler, wedged their way into the crowded room.

"And—Hooty Hoo!" a voice shouted. "Don't forget us! The gang's all here!" Christina and Grant yelped as their mom and dad entered the office, as well.

"YAYYYYYYY!" shouted Grant. "We can go home for Christmas after all!"

22

HO, HO, HO!

But that's not how it happened. The South Carolina roads were closed for the biggest snowstorm ever. Papa arranged for them all to stay at the same hotel. They celebrated Mimi's birthday with a big red and green Christmas cake. The next day they went on a shopping spree [but they didn't buy mittens, for in Mimi's consternation at Saks, she had bought at least two pair for everyone, and extras, to boot!] and later went sledding.

Papa arranged for a local restaurant to cook a Christmas Eve feast just for them, and they had a Christmas Day picnic in the hotel the next day, where all their Christmas gifts magically appeared beneath the hotel's beautiful and gigantic tree.

Speaking of magically, Agent Moo, Ashley, Cooper, and their grandmother from Columbia, who had gotten to town just before the roads closed, joined them for the entire holiday, which made it ever so much more special.

"I just still don't understand everything," Mimi said, as they drank cocoa among heaps of opened presents, looking out at the last of the snowstorm.

Agent Moo had spent part of the holiday at the police station. "Well, John Dalton talked Miss Lonesome into his scheme," she explained. "He had her give Aunt Lulu extra medication and keep her sedated upstairs in the law office. She had no family locally, which Miss Lonesome found out when she first came to work there and Lawyer Tradd was helping her get her will in order."

"And she gave Mr. Tradd more medication, too?" guessed Christina.

"That's right," said Agent Moo. "He kept it in his desk drawer, so she had about convinced him that he was getting senile. She and John Dalton just needed to keep the old folks quiet a few days while they spirited the artifacts off to Arizona...in an old antique coffin Mr. Tradd had in the back office."

"And so when we showed up looking for Aunt Lulu, they had to hide her, too?" asked Christina.

"It was mean to put that obituary in the paper," grumbled Grant.

"It was all mean," said Papa. "And bad."

"Well, let's think of the good things about the holiday," pleaded Mimi. "We all have to head home tomorrow."

"But what were you kids up to all this time?" demanded Papa. "This business about clues, and scampering around Charleston in the dark and snow alone, and..."

"WHAT?" cried Christina and Grant's parents.

"Uh," Grant said, "let's remember the good stuff," Grant prompted his grandfather.

"Good job, Agent Moo!" Papa said, to change the subject. "And thank all you kids for coming down. Christmas wouldn't be the same if we weren't all together." Everyone nodded.

Suddenly the bellman and a young girl paraded in. As they swept by, she held out her hand to show off her new engagement ring.

"Goooood job!" said Papa to the bellman, with a fat wink.

"Well, Happy Birthday, Mimi!" cried Avery.

"And Merry Christmas, everyone!" cried Ella.

"Googoogaga, hohoho!" squealed baby Evan.

"We'll miss you, Ashley and Cooper," Christina said.

Agent Moo looked puzzled. "Our names are Anna and Rebecca," the girls said together. They gave their mom a "What do you expect from a detective's kids?" look and shrug. "Ashley and Cooper are Charleston Rivers—and our secret code names."

"GRANNNNT?" shouted Papa.

"PAAAAAPA!" Grant shouted back. "I didn't have anything to do with that, really!"

Suddenly Lawyer Tradd and Aunt Lulu paraded into the room arm in arm.

"I thought you were napping," Mimi said, surprised.

"No," said Aunt Lulu with a big smile. "I was getting married!"

Everyone gasped as she showed off a gigantic heirloom diamond ring.

"WHAT?!" squealed Mimi, running to hug her aunt.

"Oh, it's easy when you are marrying a lawyer," Aunt Lulu said spryly. "And, besides, we are not spring chickens, you know, so we didn't see any reason to wait around! And, as has been said, the rumors of my death have been greatly exaggerated."

"You used to be a Spring Chicken?" Grant asked, puzzled.

When everyone else laughed, Grant crossed his arms and frowned.

"Well, just tell me what it means!" he demanded.

Papa patted him on the head. "It's just another one of those Christmas secrets, Grant."

"No more secrets!" shouted Mimi, appalled.

"No more mysteries!!" reminded Agent Moo, sternly.

"Well," said Christina, with a secret grin to the other kids. "Uh, maybe next year?!"

Rescued for Christmas!

Now...go to

www.carolemarshmysteries.com
and...

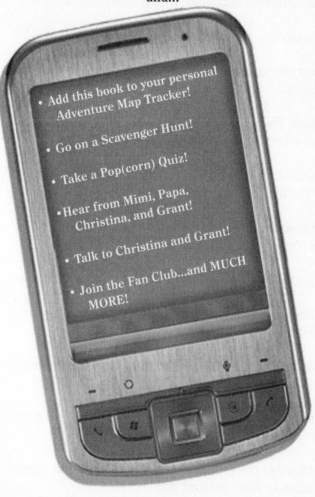

- Add this book to your personal Adventure Map Tracker!

- Go on a Scavenger Hunt!

- Take a Pop(corn) Quiz!

- Hear from Mimi, Papa, Christina, and Grant!

- Talk to Christina and Grant!

- Join the Fan Club...and MUCH MORE!

GLOSSARY

abolitionist: someone who wanted to end slavery

bombard: to hit many times

carpetbagger: a Northerner who went to the South to make a profit after the Civil War

Civil War: the war between the northern and southern states between 1861 and 1865

Gullah: a community of African American people who live in South Carolina and Georgia

impasse: a situation that one cannot get out of or escape

parapet: a wall around a fort used for protection

Reconstruction Era: the five years after the Civil War when southern states were rebuilding

secede: to break away from; southern states wanted to secede from the Union

siege: surrounding and attacking a fort or city to force surrender

slavery: the practice of owning people and forcing them to work without pay

SAT GLOSSARY

amputate: to cut off, such as a body part

bleak: desolate

defend: to take up for someone, to protect someone or something

enormous: gigantic

reluctant: unwilling

BUILT-IN BOOK CLUB
TALK ABOUT IT!

1. What would it be like to live at Fort Sumter during the Civil War?

2. Think about artifacts that have been stolen in this story. If you could have an artifact from Fort Sumter or Charleston, what would it be? Why did you pick that?

3. How would you like to visit Charleston at Christmas? Which decorations would you like to have at your house?

4. The Gullahs painted their doors blue to ward off evil. If you could paint your front door any color, what color would you choose? Why?

5. If you were living during the Civil War, what historical figure would you want to meet? Why?

6. What would you do if you were on the battlefield and you saw your brother or sister fighting on the other side? Would you help them if they were wounded?

7. Imagine you were at Fort Sumter before the first shot was fired. What would you like to say to the generals of both armies?

8. What would you buy with a ten-dollar bill in a bookstore?

9. Describe how you would feel in the middle of a battle, with cannonballs flying around you and soldiers shooting at each other? What would you do?

10. What is your favorite part of the mystery? Why?

BUILT-IN BOOK CLUB
BRING IT TO LIFE!

1. Game Day! Select three volunteers to play a game similar to "Jeopardy." Ask three other book club members to write three questions each about the mystery. Give the volunteers a "clicker" to use when they want to answer the question. Select a host to ask the questions, and see who wins!

2. Write down the names of all of the characters in the mystery on slips of paper. Fold the slips, and put them in a box. Ask each book club member to select a slip of paper from the box. Each member should then answer the following questions as if they were the character they selected. What part of the

story is your favorite and why? What makes you so important to the story? Then ask other book club members, "Who am I?"

3. Find a map and pictures of Fort Sumter. Draw and label a diagram of Fort Sumter on a poster. Include the following: officer's quarters, hospital, location of cannons, and weapons storage places.

4. Look for recipes for food that soldiers might have eaten during the Civil War. Plan a day, and have each book club member make a dish and bring it in to share.

5. Examine drawings and pictures of a Fort Sumter cannon. Research how the cannons work. Discuss what it would have been like to fire the cannon. What would you have seen, felt, heard, and smelled while you were firing a cannon during battle?

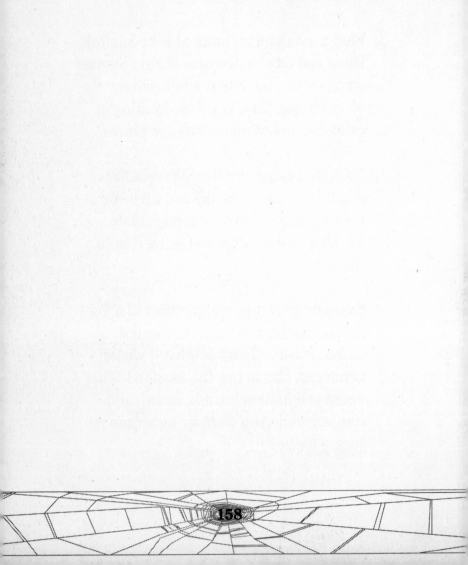